DEREK JETER

IN THE COMMUNITY

MATT ANNISS

Britannica
Educational Publishing

IN ASSOCIATION WITH

ROSEN
EDUCATIONAL SERVICES

Published in 2014 by Britannica Educational Publishing (a trademark of Encyclopædia Britannica, Inc.) in association with The Rosen Publishing Group, Inc.
29 East 21st Street, New York, NY 10010

Distributed exclusively by Rosen Publishing.
To see additional Britannica Educational Publishing titles, go to rosenpublishing.com

First Edition

Britannica Educational Publishing
J.E. Luebering: Director, Core Reference Group
Anthony L. Green: Editor, Compton's by Britannica

Rosen Publishing
Hope Lourie Killcoyne: Executive Editor
Jeanne Nagle: Senior Editor
Nelson Sá: Art Director

Library of Congress Cataloging-in-Publication Data

Derek Jeter in the community/Matt Anniss.
      pages cm.—(Making a difference: athletes who are changing the world)
Includes bibliographical references and index.
ISBN 978-1-62275-185-3 (library binding)—ISBN 978-1-62275-188-4 (pbk.)—
ISBN 978-1-62275-189-1 (6-pack)
1. Jeter, Derek, 1974—Juvenile literature. 2. Baseball players—United States—Biography—Juvenile literature. I. Title.
GV865.J48A56 2014
796.357092—dc23
[B]
                                                                                            2013024604

Manufactured in the United States of America

CONTENTS

Derek Jeter's exceptional baseball skills have made the star a sporting legend—and extremely wealthy. During the course of his MLB career, Derek has earned more than $250 million.

O f all the sports in the world, baseball is one of the toughest at which a person can excel. Anyone who has picked up a bat, pitched, caught, or fielded at shortstop—the fielding position between the second and third bases—will tell you just how difficult it can be.

Derek Jeter, shortstop for the New York Yankees, makes baseball look easy. Since joining the world-famous club as an 18-year-old in 1992, Jeter has broken countless club records, logged more than 3,000 hits, won five World Series titles, and become one of the most highly paid athletes in the world.

Jeter's off-field activities are just as astonishing. He set up his own charity in 1996, when he was just twenty-two years old, and has since given millions of dollars to good causes. The star has worked tirelessly to promote and fund programs that positively change the lives of children across the United States.

CHAPTER 1

THE STORY OF DEREK JETER

Derek Jeter (born June 26, 1974, in Pequannock, N.J.) learned a lot about discipline from an early age. His parents had met many years earlier, during their time serving in the United States Army. Derek's father and mother constantly encouraged their son to achieve, and told him that he could do anything if he worked hard enough and behaved well. Every year, his parents made Derek sign a contract that set out acceptable forms of behavior, and banned him from using the word "can't." As a result, Derek consistently focused on working hard and achieving his goals.

Determination to succeed won Derek his place as a professional baseball player with the New York Yankees.

When Derek was four years old, his family moved to Kalamazoo, Michigan. During summers spent with his grandparents in New Jersey, Derek made a number of trips to watch the New York Yankees. Inspired by the team's performances, Derek set himself the goal of becoming a professional baseball player and winning the World Series with the Yankees.

STAR STATS

Derek's father, Sanderson Charles Jeter, was a promising college baseball player. He played for Fisk University in Tennessee as a shortstop, the position Derek would later play for the Yankees.

It was during his days at Kalamazoo Central High School (above) that Derek Jeter first began to show signs of potential baseball greatness.

High School Great

In high school, Derek consistently held his team's highest batting average, and was widely thought of as one of the most promising young players in Michigan. In 1992, during his senior year at Kalamazoo Central High School, Derek received high school player of the year honors from the American Baseball Coaches Association, Gatorade, and *USA Today*. Derek seemed set for stardom.

At 18 years old, Derek faced a tough choice. He could either continue his studies while playing baseball for the University of Michigan or take his chances in the 1992 Major League Baseball (MLB) draft. In the draft, professional teams compete to sign the best high school and college players. Derek chose to enter the draft, and his gamble paid off when the Yankees chose him in the first round. Derek's childhood dream of playing for the New York Yankees had finally come true.

STAR STATS

In baseball, batting averages are figured out by dividing the number of pitches thrown by the number of successful hits — shots that result in a run. In his final year at high school, Derek Jeter had a batting average of .508, meaning he hit slightly more than half the pitches thrown to him.

MINOR LEAGUE STAR

Despite achieving his childhood dream by signing with the Yankees, it would be some time before Derek Jeter would make his first appearance at Yankee Stadium in New York. As a youngster signed to the Yankees, he spent an extended period in the minor leagues to develop as a player and prove his ability.

Derek's minor league career did not start well. He performed poorly in his debut for the Gulf Coast Yankees, a rookie league farm team of the Yankees based in Tampa, Florida. He failed to make a single hit in his first game.

STAR STATS

In 1994, Derek Jeter was named Minor League Player of the Year by *Baseball America* magazine, *The Sporting News*, *USA Today*, and Topps/National Association of Professional Baseball Leagues (NAPBL).

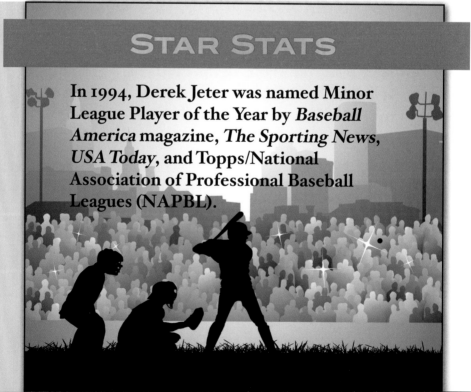

Derek's minor league career began at Legends Field (pictured here; renamed George M. Steinbrenner Field in 2008) in Florida. By the end of his season with the Gulf Coast Yankees, Derek found himself struggling at bat and doubting his ability.

Derek recovered from his shaky start in the rookie league, working his way up the farm system to become a star with the Triple A Columbus Clippers, which is the minor league team closest to the major league Yankees. He finished the 1994 season with a superb batting average. Derek was ready to join Major League Baseball.

MAJOR LEAGUE HERO

As with his minor league start, Derek's Major League Baseball career did not begin well. He failed to record a hit during his debut in May 1995, and, after 13 games, he was sent back to the minor league once more.

By the start of the 1996 season, Derek had returned to the Yankees' major league lineup. The Yankees' first rookie to start at shortstop since 1962, he soon became one of the team's

Baseball legend Derek Jeter playing for the New York Yankees at Camden Yards, home of the Baltimore (Maryland) Orioles, in 2010.

standout performers. He finished the season with a batting average of .314, including 10 home runs. These statistics helped him win, by a unanimous vote, the American League Rookie of the Year award in 1996.

From there on, things only got better for Derek. He played a vital role as the Yankees beat the Atlanta Braves by 4–2, to win the World Series. It was the first time since 1978 that the team had won the championship.

With Derek maintaining high batting and fielding averages, the Yankees became the dominant team in baseball, winning the World Series again in 1998, 1999, 2000, and 2009.

STAR STATS

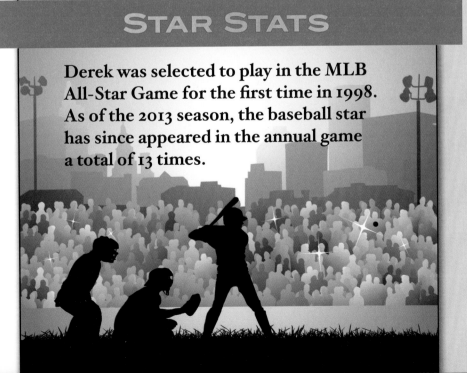

Derek was selected to play in the MLB All-Star Game for the first time in 1998. As of the 2013 season, the baseball star has since appeared in the annual game a total of 13 times.

YANKEES LEGEND

Since winning a fourth World Series in five years in 2000, the New York Yankees have struggled a bit in the offseason. However, throughout, Derek has continued to break records and win awards, sometimes despite injury. In 2009, he broke the Yankees record for the highest number of career hits, and later that year was named *Sport Illustrated* magazine's Sportsman of the Year, after leading the Yankees to another World Series win.

It hasn't always been easy for the man Yankees fans like to call "Mr. November." This is a nickname given to Derek due to his exceptional performances in the postseason playoffs, where the best teams compete for trophies at the end of the regular season. Since the mid-2000s, Derek has been criticized for the quality of his fielding, and his spells on the bench due to injury have become longer. In 2013, Derek missed three months of the regular season and the All-Star Game after injuring his ankle.

In 2011, Derek joined an elite group of 28 all-time baseball greats who have recorded at least 3,000 hits in their careers.

A Place in the Hall of Fame

No one knows how long Derek Jeter will keep playing baseball, but almost everyone agrees that a place in the Baseball Hall of Fame awaits when he finally retires.

Since starting his career as a nervous teenager in 1992, Derek has played more than 2,500 games for the Yankees. Throughout, his batting average has remained high, and his form has been consistently impressive.

Maintaining such an exceptionally high level of performance has made Derek one of the most respected players in baseball. In New York, he is nothing less than a superstar.

STAR STATS

During his career, Derek Jeter has won the Gold Glove Award for fielding five times — in 2004, 2005, 2006, 2009, and 2010.

Derek crosses the line to a delighted Yankee Stadium crowd after recording his 3,000th hit while playing against the Tampa Bay Rays in 2011. He became just the second player in Major League history to log his 3,000th hit with a home run.

Derek sets a great example off the field, too. He's become well known as a community champion, a great charity fundraiser, and an athlete who does plenty for good causes. When Derek retires from baseball, no one doubts that the star will continue to try to make a difference in the lives of those less fortunate than himself.

CHAPTER 2

SOMEWHERE
TO TURN 2

Growing up, Derek Jeter's favorite baseball player was New York Yankees outfielder Dave Winfield. Derek's bedroom wall was covered with posters of the baseball star, and Derek looked forward to his trips to Yankee Stadium to watch Winfield in action.

It wasn't Winfield's sporting feats alone that impressed Derek. The Yankees legend

Today, Derek Jeter (left) is as great a legend as his childhood hero, Dave Winfield (right). The great baseball player and committed supporter of young people provided inspiration for Derek both on and off the baseball field.

was also committed to making a difference in the lives of young people in his community.

According to the MLB Web site, Derek turned to his father and said: "If I make it to the Major Leagues, I want to set up a foundation that will have a positive impact on kids. I want to help nurture dreams. I want to show kids there's another way to go."

Derek was as good as his word. Since the early years of his New York Yankees career, he has committed considerable time and funds to his charity, the Turn 2 Foundation. (The name incorporates his Yankee jersey number.) Each year, the charity changes the lives of thousands of young people across the United States.

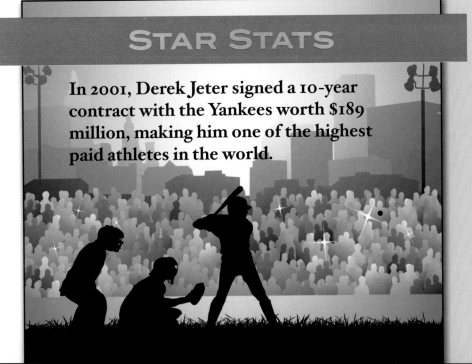

STAR STATS

In 2001, Derek Jeter signed a 10-year contract with the Yankees worth $189 million, making him one of the highest paid athletes in the world.

IN THE BEGINNING

In 1996, Derek was 22 years old, and had just enjoyed an outstanding rookie season with the Yankees. Many athletes would simply be taking time to enjoy their success, but Derek was ready to make a difference in his community.

Over the course of a few hours, Derek and his father planned how his charity would work. They figured out how it would operate and how they would fund it through a mixture of Derek's own donations, fundraising events, and donations from friends and sponsors. Most importantly, they decided how they

STAR STATS

During his most successful season in 1999, Derek Jeter recorded 219 hits for 102 runs batted in, including 24 home runs.

Derek at bat against the Texas Rangers in 2003. Derek has used the wealth generated by his enormous success on the baseball field to fund his Turn 2 Foundation.

would help young people. Within a few weeks, the Turn 2 Foundation was born.

On the charity's website, Derek explained his thinking: "Giving back to my community, especially the children in those communities, is really important to me," he wrote. "By showing how I lend my support, I hope to inspire you to help out in your communities as well."

GIVING BACK

Since it was launched in 1996, Derek
Jeter's Turn 2 Foundation has donated
more than $16 million to support "signature
programs" and charities in three states:
New York, where the shortstop plays for the
Yankees; Michigan, where he grew up; and
Florida, where the sports star sharpened
his skills in the minor leagues.

Derek (center left) attends the Jeter's Leaders
Leadership Conference in Tampa in 2011, at which the
Turn 2 Foundation's aims and objectives are discussed.

From the outset, Derek Jeter had a clear idea of what he wanted the Turn 2 Foundation to achieve. According to a statement on the charity's website, Jeter's goal is to help children "grow safely and successfully into adulthood and become the leaders of tomorrow." The foundation supports organizations and programs that encourage children to lead healthy lifestyles and achieve at school and college. It also sets out to equip children with the skills they need to become community leaders, so they will go on to also set a great example in their neighborhood, school, college, or place of work in the future.

STAR STATS

In 2003, Derek was named official club captain of the New York Yankees. It is a position he still holds. Other players who have captained the Yankees include greats such as Babe Ruth, Lou Gehrig, and Don Mattingly.

The areas in which the Turn 2 Foundation works are those that personally mean a lot to Derek Jeter. The lessons taught to the baseball star by his parents, such as the importance of avoiding alcohol and drugs, working hard at school, and setting a good example form the basis of the charity's aims.

Over the years, the Turn 2 Foundation has developed a number of signature programs. Operating with the help of many volunteers, these programs promote healthy living

Derek receives a check for $100,000 from Delta Air Lines for the Turn 2 Foundation in 2009.

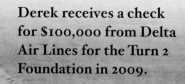

DELTA

JETER
WRIGHT
HITTING CHALLENGE

November 2009

PAY TO THE
ORDER OF _____ *Turn 2 Foundation* ___ **$100,000**

One Hundred Thousand DOLLARS

through sports, working hard at school, and the importance of saying no to alcohol and drugs.

The foundation also makes a difference by awarding money to other organizations that promote beliefs similar to its own mission. The foundation hosts special events at which Derek Jeter talks about his experiences, with the aim of inspiring young people to make positive choices in life, just as he has done.

STAR STATS

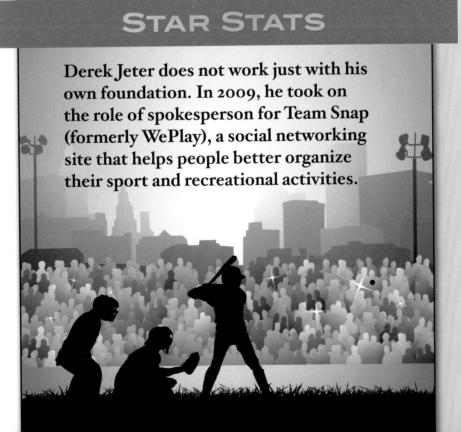

Derek Jeter does not work just with his own foundation. In 2009, he took on the role of spokesperson for Team Snap (formerly WePlay), a social networking site that helps people better organize their sport and recreational activities.

JETER'S LEADERS

The Turn 2 Foundation's best-known program is Jeter's Leaders, a long-running catalog of events designed to reward and develop the skills of high school students who set an outstanding example for those around them.

Each year, between 8 and 10 eighth grade students in New York and West Michigan are chosen to take part in the program. To be chosen, each young person must have excellent grades, live their life free of alcohol and drugs, volunteer with community groups such as local sports clubs or charities, and show a desire to be a good role model for those around them.

STAR STATS

Since 1997, almost 200 students have graduated from the Jeter's Leaders program. Most have gone to college, and volunteered with local community groups.

Jeter's Leaders are given training in leadership skills from Derek Jeter himself, and other qualified volunteers.

Those chosen to be part of the program are given support throughout high school by the charity. Participants are expected to attend summer camps and conferences, where they learn new skills that can be used to improve the lives of others in their neighborhoods. A small number of Jeter's Leaders also experience life in the workplace as part of paid summer internships with a variety of leading American companies.

THE JETER METER

As a professional athlete, Derek Jeter passionately believes in the importance of exercise as part of a healthy lifestyle. As a result, many of the Turn 2 Foundation's programs focus on encouraging youngsters to play sports and generally be more active.

One of the best programs is The Jeter Meter in New York, which runs after-school activity clubs at community centers in the Bronx, Queens, Brooklyn, and Manhattan. Children under ten years of age are encouraged to walk and run more often, both in their day-to-day lives and by training for short "fun runs."

STAR STATS

In the 2012-13 school year, between them, children who took part in The Jeter Meter program ran or walked an amazing 8,465 miles (13,623 km).

As part of The Jeter Meter, each child is given a goal, which during the 2012-13 school year was to walk or run the equivalent of a marathon, which is 26.2 miles (42 km). Children are given Jeter Meter cards to keep track of their progress. When they hit their goals, they are rewarded with prizes such as t-shirts and medals. In 2012-13, more than 300 children in New York took part in the program.

Children running along an outdoor path. The Jeter Meter program encourages kids to walk, run, and generally make exercise and activity a part of their daily lives.

PROUD 2 BE ME

In West Michigan, another of the Turn 2 Foundation's signature programs is helping fourth-, fifth-, and sixth-graders to withstand the pressure in their community to turn to alcohol and drugs. Proud 2 Be Me is one of Derek Jeter's favorite programs. It is an after-school club that offers youngsters various fun projects, including sports and learning activities, as well as advice from older members of the Jeter's Leaders program.

Like many of the other Turn 2 Foundation programs, the project aims to teach children the importance of leading a healthy lifestyle, working hard at school, helping others, and setting the right example.

Every year, students take part in many different activities. In November 2012, they spent the month making blankets, which were presented to local senior citizens during the holiday season. They also helped out at their schools, assisting teachers in any way they could. Earlier in the year, participants took classes in the martial art of taekwondo, and were taken to see a ballet. Other activities children have enjoyed include a visit to the Mayors' Riverfront Park in Kalamazoo and a trip to Washington, D.C.

In December 2012, Derek and other New York Yankees met with more than 600 children at Yankee Stadium. As part of the holiday celebration, Derek helped hand out presents to the children.

31

TURN 2 US

Many of the programs started and paid for by Derek Jeter's Turn 2 Foundation are based around after-school programs, conducted either at schools or in community centers.

In 2001, Jeter joined forces with Morgan Stanley Children's Hospital of New York-Presbyterian and a local public school to launch Turn 2 Us. This program is designed to foster healthy minds and bodies in elementary schoolchildren.

The program has been very successful since it first launched. Every year, it holds an annual "father-child night" for students and

STAR STATS

During the course of his Yankees career, shortstop Derek Jeter has made just 242 fielding errors, the equivalent of 13 per season.

The Turn 2 Us program encourages children to lead active lifestyles and adopt healthy diets. The program also reinforces the benefits of working hard at school, and setting and trying to achieve goals.

their fathers, attended by between 50 and 60 families. The program also funds after-school basketball and baseball leagues, and teaches children how to deal with people who might offer them alcohol or drugs.

The program continues through the school summer vacation. Most years, Turn 2 Us runs a sports and arts summer camp in New York. There, students play sports, dance, learn how to cook, and visit museums.

TOMORROW'S LEADERS

Since launching the Turn 2 Foundation in 1996, Derek Jeter has attempted to support programs that give schoolchildren of all ages the chance to better themselves and achieve all that they can in life. One of the ways the

Derek has often spoken of his belief that children are "tomorrow's leaders." The star aims to encourage and reward those who work hard and show talent at school.

Turn 2 Foundation encourages children is by offering scholarships to promising students. As with the Jeter's Leaders program, students can only apply for a scholarship if they achieve great grades, help their community, and show that they lead a healthy lifestyle.

At present, Derek Jeter's Turn 2 Foundation currently funds five scholarship programs. One of these helps 15 students each year attend the St. Peter Claver Catholic School in Florida. The others pay for teenagers in New York, West Michigan, New Jersey, and Florida to go to college.

STAR STATS

Over the length of his Major League Baseball career, Derek Jeter has had more than 10,550 at-bats.

CHAPTER 4

LEADING BY EXAMPLE

From the very beginning of his career, Derek Jeter has tried to set a good example for others, particularly the youngsters who view the star as a hero. In interviews, Derek has spoken of his desire to inspire others to live their lives positively and approach tasks with a "can do" attitude.

On the baseball field, Derek is the Yankees "go-to" man and club captain. Whenever the team has needed him the most, whether in regular season games, play offs, or the

Along with working hard to further his own foundation, Derek is also an active supporter of other charities.

World Series, Derek has responded with an amazing catch, stop, hit, or home run.

Off the baseball field, Derek also tries to inspire, either through his charity work or his public speaking events. The star is also passionate about encouraging children to play baseball. Every year, the Turn 2 Foundation runs four-day baseball coaching clinics at recreation centers in New York, West Michigan, and Florida. Jeter attends the clinics to head some of the coaching sessions and talk to children about leading a healthy lifestyle.

STAR STATS

Derek Jeter has won the Hank Aaron Award twice, in 2006 and 2009. The award is presented each year to the MLB top hitter, and is voted for by both fans and journalists.

FAMILY AFFAIR

Ever since he was a youngster growing up in Kalamazoo, Michigan, Derek Jeter has believed in the importance of family. He has never forgotten the love and support he got from his parents and sister, Sharlee, throughout his childhood and the difficult days of his early baseball career. Needing reassurance during his first season in the minor leagues, Derek spent $400 a month on phone calls to his parents.

When Derek decided to set up the Turn 2 Foundation in 1996, he turned to his family for help. Both his parents had set a good example for Derek during his childhood, volunteering with various local community groups. Both now sit on the board of the Turn 2 Foundation.

The Jeters take great pride in Derek's foundation, and share his passion for helping children make the most of their talents.

"Derek wants to set a good example, he wants to be a role model," his father has written on the foundation's website. "Seeing that, as his father, I'm extremely proud."

Derek's sister Sharlee (center left) acts as president of the Turn 2 Foundation. Sharlee earned her presidency by working as a volunteer for the foundation throughout her years in college.

A SHINING EXAMPLE

Athletes are often viewed as great role models for the example they set on the field. However, not all athletes can claim to be great role models both on the field and off it. There are often press stories about high-profile athletes who behave badly in their free time, and who do not set a good example for young people who might be influenced by their actions.

Derek Jeter is a genuinely great role model. Despite some on-field setbacks early in his career, he recovered and became stronger from the experience.

STAR STATS

Derek Jeter has played one game against his own team, the New York Yankees. He played for the United States National Team when they beat the Yankees in an exhibition game in Tampa, Florida, in 2009.

Derek is hugely popular with the American public because of his exemplary behavior both on and off the field. The star's achievements in his baseball career and his charity work are remarkable. Derek is well behaved, ambitious, and hard working. Few athletes set a better example for young people today.

Derek's commitment to his team and his charity work is unfailing. His dedication to both his sport and his charitable causes sets a superb example for young people.

COMMUNITY HERO

As one of the most consistent performers of his generation, and with many records and awards to his name, Derek Jeter is considered one of baseball's all-time greats and a living legend in the sport.

The star's contributions to the lives of thousands of young people in the U.S. has made him a legend off the baseball field, too. Through the Turn 2 Foundation, many youngsters have been turned away from alcohol and drugs, learned the benefits of a healthy lifestyle, and focused on achieving at school.

In 2011, Jeter was invited back to Kalamazoo Central High School, where he first shone on the baseball field, to talk to students. The school was so proud of Derek's achievements and his contribution to the community that they re-named their baseball field in his honor. It was a perfect tribute to an athlete who will be remembered not only for his great career, but also for his outstanding contribution to the lives of so many people.

Derek Jeter has become one of the most famous sports stars of his age. Derek is an outstanding athlete who has made an inspirational difference to his community.

1992: Derek graduates from high school and signs with the New York Yankees.

1994: He enjoys an excellent season with the Triple A Columbus Clippers.

1995: In May, Derek makes his Major League Baseball debut for the New York Yankees. He struggles and is sent back to the minor leagues.

1996: He returns to the Yankees and enjoys an excellent season. Derek is named American League Rookie of the Year after picking up first-place votes from all 28 judges.

1996: Derek launches the Turn 2 Foundation.

1998: The star is selected for the MLB All-Star Game for the first time. He finishes third in voting for the American League Most Valuable Player Award.

2000: Derek is named Most Valuable Player in the MLB All-Star Game and the World Series MVP.

2001: Derek signs a 10-year professional contract worth $189 million with the New York Yankees.

2004: He wins the prestigious Gold Glove Award for best fielding for the first time in his career.

2009: Derek sets a new Yankees club record for the highest number of career hits.

2009: The star breaks a number of long-standing Yankees and MLB records on his way to another World Series win, the fifth of his career.

2010: Derek signs a new three-year deal with the Yankees.

2011: He becomes the 28th Major League Baseball player to record 3,000 career hits during regular season games.

2013: After missing part of the 2012 season due to an ankle injury, Derek returns to action for the Yankees after the All-Star break.

Kevin Durant
The National Basketball Association (NBA) and Olympic Team USA basketball star has raised money for various charities, including a $1 million donation to the America Red Cross to help victims of the Oklahoma City tornado in 2013.

Jeff Gordon
The leading National Association for Stock Car Auto Racing (NASCAR) driver works tirelessly to raise money for cancer charities.

Robert Griffin III
The pro football player began volunteering for a number of charities while in college.

Mia Hamm
The leading soccer player's Mia Hamm Foundation raises money for families of children suffering from rare diseases.

Tony Hawk
The skateboarding legend's charity, The Tony Hawk Foundation, has provided more than $3.4 million to build 400 skate parks around the United States.

Magic Johnson
The NBA legend founded the Magic Johnson Foundation in 1991, to fund a range of educational projects. Today, 250,000 young Americans benefit from its funded projects every year.

Peyton and Eli Manning
The record-breaking Super Bowl MVP brothers support many causes through fundraising, including the work of the PeyBack Foundation, the charity set up by Peyton Manning.

Kurt Warner
The former Super Bowl MVP's First Things First Foundation improves the lives of impoverished children.

Venus and Serena Williams
The record-breaking tennis players devote huge amounts of time to charity. They are also fearless campaigners for equal rights for women.

campaigners People who carry out work with the aim of achieving a specific goal, such as raising money for charity.

community A group of people in one particular area.

contract A written agreement between two or more people.

debut A first appearance.

donations Money or objects given to a charity or organization.

drugs Dangerous, harmful, and illegal substances.

fund To give money, usually to a charity group, to carry out a project.

fundraiser A person who raises money for charity.

home run Hitting the ball far enough to run around all four bases on the baseball diamond, scoring a run.

leaders People who organize or inspire others.

MLB Major League Baseball, the organization that oversees the American League, National League, postseason playoffs, and World Series.

playoffs Winner-takes all games. In playoffs, only the winners progress to play the next match. For the losers, their season is over.

postseason The period of playoffs that begins following the completion of the regular season, featuring only the best teams in the competition.

promote To encourage an interest in something.

retires Stops performing a role or a job.

role model A person whose good behavior and attitude inspires others.

rookie A player in their first year as a professional athlete.

scholarships Monies won by students in order to study.

shortstop A fielding position in baseball between second and third base.

sponsors People who give money to an athlete or team in order to be associated with their success.

taekwondo A martial art that involves hitting and kicking an opponent to score points.

Books

Christopher, Matt and Glenn Stout. *The New York Yankees* (Legendary Sports Teams). New York, NY: Little, Brown Group, 2008.

Edwards, Ethan. *Meet Derek Jeter: Baseball's Superstar Shortstop* (All Star Players). New York, NY: PowerKids Press, 2008.

Marcovitz, Hal. *Derek Jeter* (Modern Role Models). Broomall, PA: Mason Crest, 2008.

Robinson, Tom. *Derek Jeter: Captain On and Off the Field* (Sports Stars With Heart). Berkeley Heights, NJ: Enslow Publishers, 2009.

Roth, B. A. *Derek Jeter: A Yankee Hero* (All Aboard Reading). New York, NY: Grosset & Dunlap, 2009.

Websites

Due to the changing nature of Internet links, Rosen Publishing has developed an online list of Websites related to the subject of this book. This site is updated regularly. Please use this link to access the list:

http://www.rosenlinks.com/mad/jeter